Love,
Amy

For all the children who are famous to someone
that loves them, especially Miranda and Brandon.
—B.B.

For Mom.
—Y.C.

IMPRINT
A part of Macmillan Publishing Group, LLC
175 Fifth Avenue, New York, NY 10010

ABOUT THIS BOOK
The artist's medium is pencil and digital. The text was set in Brandon Grotesque
and the display type is Frontage. The book was edited by Erin Stein and art directed by
Natalie C. Sousa. The production was supervised by Raymond Ernesto Colón,
and the production editor was Dawn Ryan.

Printed in China by Toppan Leefung Printing Ltd.,
Dongguan City, Guangdong Province

Library of Congress Cataloging-in-Publication Data is available.

ISBN 978-1-250-13490-5

Our books may be purchased in bulk for promotional, educational, or business use. Please
contact your local bookseller or the Macmillan Corporate and Premium Sales Department
at (800) 221-7945 ext. 5442 or by e-mail at MacmillanSpecialMarkets@macmillan.com.

Book design by Liz Casal
Imprint logo designed by Amanda Spielman

First edition, 2019

1 3 5 7 9 10 8 6 4 2

mackids.com

Beware of the book thief, destined to be
famous for all the wrong reasons.

BARBARA BOTTNER

AMY

IS

FAMOUS

Lucy, a Ladybug
was pretty and kind,
but not all the time.
Amy

ILLUSTRATED BY YUYI CHEN

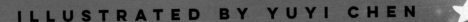

[Imprint]
MAKE YOUR MARK

New York

Last week, Miss Anna gave me
a star for my poem.

This week, she gave me a star for the drawing I did of Bear, my best friend. Miss Anna says, "Stars for a star!"

I want to stay famous,
so I write more poems and draw more pictures.

I pose for a photo with my mom and dad.
They knew me before I was famous.

Next, I sign autographs. When you're a star, you're too busy
to write your whole name. I write just an *A* for *Amy*.

I tell Bear, "Stars are famous people! I must be famous!"

Bear says she doesn't understand.

"When you're extra good at things, you get to
be on magazine covers," I explain.
"And you get to be on TV shows and in movies.
And everyone says you are the most important person."

Bear doesn't care about being famous. She likes snuggles.
I like snuggles, too, but I like being famous even more.

Famous people wear red, so I wear my red dress,
red headband, and red socks to school.

Miss Anna says we should welcome the new girl, Cecile.
She's dressed like Hermione Granger, from the Harry Potter movie.

"Why are you dressed like that?" I ask.

"I love Harry Potter. Don't you?" says Cecile.
"Anyway, my mother knows a famous actress who gave me
the actual scarf from the movie."

Miranda, Nicole, and Daisy rush over and touch the scarf.
"How does it feel to be famous?" they ask her.

"Cecile wasn't *in* the movie," I explain.
"She doesn't know Emma Watson! So who cares?"

Cecile says,
"I wasn't trying to be famous. . .
but, I think I like it."

She waves to everyone as if she's the queen.

"Why are you waving?" I ask.

"I'm just saying hi to all my new fans," she whispers.

Miss Anna asks Cecile to help me hand out the
cookies during reading time even though I don't need any help.

Cecile's talking again.

"*Shhhh*! We are supposed to be quiet when
we hand out cookies," I explain.

There can't be *two* famous people in one tiny classroom!

At bedtime, I close the curtains.
Bear and I wear plain pajamas.

I go to sleep dreaming that Cecile's
parents have found her a different school
where she can be famous all by herself.

Then, the only famous person
will be *me*, again.

In the morning, I wear mostly muddy colors.

"You and Bear look glum," says my mom.

"We are. That's why I'm taking her to school. Even famous people need a best friend."

Bear says she doesn't like Cecile.

Mom tells Bear that Cecile's the new girl and she's just trying to fit in.

Today, Cecile is wearing a headband
with a red bow and cat ears.

"I'm dressed like Hello Kitty," she tells us.
"My mother is friends with Kitty's mother."

"I think Hello Kitty is from Japan," I say.

Nicole whispers that she thinks she saw Cecile on TV last night!
Everyone asks Cecile for her autograph.

"Cecile wasn't on TV!" I tell them.
"She just wears stupid costumes."

"You're just jealous," says Nicole.

Bear cries. I tell Bear that famous people don't cry.
Still, they can have a bad day.

The next day, Cecile's wearing all red! Red is *my* color!
"Why are you dressed in red?" I ask her.

"Famous people wear red."

Bear says Cecile is a copycat. Why would she copy me?

I take another look at Cecile. Maybe Mom is right.
Maybe Cecile is just a new girl who wants to have friends.

Today, it's Saturday. My mom says I have a playdate.

The front door opens. Someone is dressed *exactly* like Annie from the musical. Guess who?

"Can you sing?" I ask Cecile.

"Not a note," she says.

"Well, want to plant some seeds?"

"Celebrities don't touch dirt," says Cecile.

"Want to paint butterflies on our faces?"

"No, I have to always look pretty for my fans," says Cecile.
"How about we play photo shoot? Take my picture."

After that we just sit and stare at each other.

"I'm not having any fun," Cecile finally admits.

"Me neither," I say.

"When you're famous, you have to smile even when you are sad," she says. "And the clothes scratch."

"I know!" I agree. "Signing autographs makes
your hand hurt, too."

"I just want to be a regular girl," Cecile says.

"Me too!"

I lend Cecile my pink shorts and we hunt for frogs.

We drink our milk together and finish
at exactly the same time.

I try on her Annie costume. It *is* scratchy!

Bear says she's changed her mind about Cecile,
and we invite her to stay for dinner.

On Monday, I tell Cecile we should be famous,
but only to each other.
So, we're both regular girls now.

It turns out regular girls get the
exact same number of hugs as famous girls.

Or even more.